The Cheetah Who Ran Too Fast

and other children's stories from Africa

Written and illustrated by
TRUDI FRANKE

PENGUIN BOOKS

PENGUIN BOOKS

Published by the Penguin Group
Penguin Books (South Africa) (Pty) Ltd, 24 Sturdee Avenue, Rosebank, Johannesburg 2196,
South Africa
Penguin Books Ltd, 80 Strand, London WC2R 0RL, England
Penguin Group (USA) Inc, 375 Hudson Street, New York, New York 10014, USA
Penguin Group (Canada), 90 Eglinton Avenue East, Suite 700, Toronto, Ontario, M4P 2Y3,
Canada (a division of Pearson Penguin Canada Inc.)
Penguin Ireland, 25 St Stephen's Green, Dublin 2, Ireland (a division of Penguin Books Ltd)
Penguin Group (Australia), 250 Camberwell Road, Camberwell, Victoria 3124, Australia
(a division of Pearson Australia Group Pty Ltd)
Penguin Books India Pvt Ltd, 11 Community Centre, Panchsheel Park, New Delhi – 110 017,
India
Penguin Group (NZ), 67 Apollo Drive, Mairangi Bay, Auckland 1310, New Zealand
(a division of Pearson New Zealand Ltd)

Penguin Books (South Africa) (Pty) Ltd, Registered Offices:
24 Sturdee Avenue, Rosebank, Johannesburg 2196, South Africa

www.penguinbooks.co.za

First published by Wild African Publishers 2003
Reprinted 2005
This edition published by Penguin Books (South Africa) (Pty) Ltd 2009

Copyright text © Trudi Franke 2003
Copyright illustrations © Trudi Franke 2005

ISBN: 978-0-143-02607-5

Typeset by CJH Design in 12/15 pt Clarendon
Cover design: Flame Design
Printed and bound by Interpak Books, Pietermaritzburg

For Paul, David and Owen

Contents

Making a difference

These 'Teach and Learn' African stories are tools for Parents, Grandparents and other Special People to teach children life skills and values.

They should be read out loud, with as much expression as the reader can muster to convey their suspense, emotion and laughter.

More importantly, however, these stories have been written to inspire moments of deeper interaction between reader and child, to build relationships, and to teach children about real life values like empathy, compassion, understanding and kindness.

At home, or in the playground, our children have a great deal to learn. In a constantly changing world, they are faced with ever increasing challenges. It is up to us, as Parents, Grandparents and Special People alike, to look for those moments, those opportunities, to teach children about taking responsibility and learning how to deal with these challenges in a positive and meaningful way that will promote their confidence and a healthy self-image.

If we can make a difference in our children's lives, then the future, and our children in that future, will grow stronger and brighter from generation to generation.

What a legacy!

The Cheetah Who Ran Too Fast

About taking things one step at a time

Cheetah is the fastest we all know that
He goes from 0 to 100 ks in two seconds flat
Fastest by far without even a push
The fastest animal in the African bush

But …
The problem with Cheetah was
– although he was fast –
His memory
of where
he should go
did not last

He'd be asked to go this way
then that way to fetch such
It wouldn't be a big deal
It wouldn't be asking too much
And he'd shoot off fast
with the very best of intention
(He did mean well
it's fair to mention)

But somewhere along
it would all
start to crumble
The where
and the how
and the why
would all jumble

His eyes
would cross over
His brain
would start burning
His fur
would stand upright
His stomach
start churning

And he'd
zoom around
like a small spotted Boeing
Unable to remember
where he was going

He'd zig this way ...
and zag that
all over the place
Growing more
and more
red in the face

With all the directions
spinning round in his head
He'd land up
somewhere else instead

So all the animals
of the bushveld knew
that Cheetah
could not
see it through

When he was asked
to fetch or to find
they knew
he would simply
lose track
in his mind

Poor Cheetah
would often
go off to cry
Because
nobody trusted him
and he knew why

From his eyes
to his nose
his fur
became dark
As the tears
that he cried
left a
permanent mark

Now it happened one day ...

Young Elephant decided
not to follow the rest
of his family down to the wallow
He decided rather to dilly and dally
to the shady mud pool way down in the valley

And he didn't tell anyone where he was going
He slipped off quietly without anyone knowing

Which
as we all know
is not very wise
As the African bush
is full of surprise

And you never know just
what there could be
waiting around
in the bushes, you see

But luckily ... this day
Cheetah was there
lying and crying
whilst cleaning his hair

He watched
Young Elephant
come down
to the pool
And start to roll
in the muddy cool

And
as he watched
he saw Elephant
become still ...
But he didn't
think anything
of it until ...

He noticed
that Elephant
could only
blink
And slowly ...
as he watched
Elephant began
to ... sink!

There he was, a muddy heap
Stuck in the mud really deep
And sinking a little, bit ... by bit ...
Now what was Cheetah
going to do about it?

Well Cheetah at once started to
panic
His brain spun and his face went all
manic

But then quite suddenly ...
out of the blue ...
A clear thought popped up
and he knew
exactly what ...
he had ... to do

He had to find help
A big Elephant brother
a father, a sister
an Elephant mother

So he asked
Young Elephant
where they all were

With a muddy reply
Elephant said
he was sure

They were all
at the wallow
next to the river

But as he heard the directions
Cheetah started to shiver

Said Elephant ... (muddily)
'Go first to the green tree
up on the hill
Then round the big boulder
travel right until
You come to an anthill shaped
like an arrow
Then go down the path
straight and narrow'

'Cross over the river, and a little more
To the Elephants' wallow on the opposite shore'

Now this all sounds easy
to you or me
But to Cheetah, well …
it just wouldn't be

His head went all wonky
His brain became fried
And he couldn't remember
He tried, tried and tried

So we must think of something
and think of it fast
To help Cheetah change
his directionless past

SO SHOUT OUT LOUD
SHOUT OUT WITH ME

'Cheetah!'

'Cheetah!'

'Go straight
to the
green tree!'

Cheetah stopped in mid spin
It all became clear
He moved his legs into first gear
And shot off like a bullet
Oh what a thrill
To the green tree ... the green tree
The green tree on the hill

But when he reached the green tree
his brain started to fail
And he couldn't remember
the rest of the trail

Come on, everyone,
we must let him know
Which direction
he has got to go!

'Go around the
big boulder
Then to the
right'

Off went Cheetah
at the speed of light

But by now Young
Elephant's
situation was dire

And to make matters worse
He was starting
to tire ...
So further
into the mud
he sunk
'til all
you could see
were his tusks ...
and his trunk ...

But our Cheetah
was still going
full steam ahead
Without hesitation
he went
where we led

'Straight to
the anthill
shaped
like an arrow
Then on to the path,
straight and narrow ...
Now cross over the river
and a
little more ...
To the
Elephants'
wallow on the
opposite shore'

And Cheetah did just that
At 120 kilometres flat
He reached the Elephants
at the wallow
And shouted loudly
for them to follow

'Young Elephant is in very big trouble
You must come now!
Quick!
on the double!'

The elephants rushed all the way
to where the young elephant lay

The rest of him
had already
sunk

Now all
you could see
was the
tip of his trunk!

Mother Elephant
grabbed it
and started
to pull
Then Father
Then Sister
Then
Big Brother Bull

They pulled ... and pulled
each behind the other

The Mother ...
the Father ...
the Sister ...
the Brother ...

And then
came Cheetah
pulling with
all his might

Our Cheetah who finally
HAD GOT IT RIGHT!
He'd followed directions
one step at a time
And that's how
young Elephant was able to climb

Slowly ... but surely ... bit ... by bit
Out of the muddy, muddy pit

That night
the whole
of the African
animal nation
Came together
in
great celebration

And Cheetah was
a hero
A bright shining
star

The fastest and bravest
Cheetah by far

And of course, now EVERYONE
knew that ...
(with a bit of good luck)

NUDGE, NUDGE
WINK, WINK

Cheetah COULD help them
If they were stuck

WHAT IS THIS STORY ABOUT?
What does it say?

Well ...
when you are asked to
follow directions
Or maybe to answer some
difficult questions

Take it first one step
then two ... then three ...
And you'll finish the task
correctly

And remember ...
Some will work slowly
Some will work fast
Some will come first
and
Some will come last

But one step at a time
and you'll pass any test

We are ALL heroes when we
try our best

Two Wild Dogs

About listening to wise words

In the African bush
under the African sun
Lived two young Wild Dogs
who enjoyed having fun

They stayed quite happily
inside their den
And would go outside
with their parents
now and then

Their mother and father
would keep them safe and sound
Until they returned to their den
underground

But Wild Dog parents
have to hunt for food
And they asked their pups to stay inside
and be good

They would say . . .

'If you go outside
there are dangers around
It's best if you stay
right here, underground'

'There are lions and crocodiles
leopards and snakes

Ditches and mud holes
rivers and lakes'

'So stay in the den,
we'll be back by noon
Stay safe in the den,
we'll be back quite soon'

Now WE all know
that parents are clever
when they tell us
behave, be safe and never
go out on your own
without them knowing
just WHERE
and
WITH WHOM
you are going

So we hope our
pups listen
and stay
underground
Safe from those
dangers
all around

We hope that
they listen
And do as
they're told
We hope that
they will
NOT
be too bold

And go outside
where they should not
Under the African sun, so hot

BUT ...

Oh NO!

LOOK, LOOK!

Our Wild Dogs have NOT listened
and are starting to creep
Up out of the den
to take a peep

What if WE warned them
do you think they would stop
Let's give it a try
before they get to the top

'Don't go outside, there
are dangers are around
It's best if you stay safe
underground'

'There are lions and
crocodiles
leopards and snakes
Ditches and mud holes
rivers and lakes'

'So listen to your parents
and do as you're told'

'Do NOT go out there!
Do NOT be so bold!'

But they say
'Our parents just fuss
And they would not listen
not even to us'

So up they creep
as close as can be
To the outside
and they see

The mud holes ARE muddy
the ditches ARE deep
Still further out
they begin to creep

The rivers ARE running
The lakes wide and wet
But no other dangers
can they see as yet

Still further ...
and further ...
and further
they go out

No other
dangers
seem
round about ...

THEN ...

The lion pounces!   POUNCE!
  The crocodile snaps!   SNAP!
The leopard leaps!   LEAP!
  The snake springs!   SPRING!

(PAUSE)

Oh what has happened?

What do you think?

Well quick, quick, quick as a wink
Our two Wild Dogs
shot back underground
Back to their den
safe and sound

And NEVER again
will they go out
without their parents
round about

WHAT IS THIS STORY ABOUT?
What does it say?

Our parents just fuss, so it would seem
But really deep down, we know what they mean
We know that they care for us and are clever
When they tell us to behave, be safe and never
Go out on our own without them knowing
Just WHERE and WITH WHOM you are going

Parents love us completely, full up and much more
And don't want us harmed or even made heart sore
So we SHOULD listen to what they say
To keep safe and to stay away
From unsafe places and talking to strangers
Crossing roads and other such dangers

The dos the don'ts, the YOU SHOULD NOTS
About electric sockets and hot cooking pots
Are there to keep you safe and sound
From all the dangerous things around

The Toothless Lion

About standing together and caring for each other

Mavimba was a Lion,
I'm told,
Who was not as wise
as he was bold

He had lost all his teeth
in a fearsome battle
His skin-and-bone body
had begun to rattle

As he lay down
in the shade to rest
A Hoopoe bird spoke
from up high in her nest

'Mavimba is old
and not very strong
I must stay here and make sure
nothing goes wrong'

'For if Sheevah finds him here
I am afraid
He'll not last the day,
his fate will be made'

Along came Lumka
the jungle hare
He came to see
Mavimba,
as close
as he dare

He watched
his old friend
breathing
in and out
His old friend
the Lion,
no longer stout

'I must stay by his
side,
in case he must hide

For if Sheevah
finds him here
I am afraid
He'll not last the day,
his fate will be made'

Along came the
old Elephant
Andukha's
his name
With gigantic
white tusks
that speak of
his fame

He looked down at
Mavimba,
all tattered and worn
He remembered the
day
when Mavimba was
born

'I must stand over
Mavimba
and give him more
shade,
'til the heat of
the day
begins to fade'

And many a bird,
animal and insect

Gathered near Mavimba
to watch and protect

So when Sheevah arrived
with a glint in his eye
So many were there
that none could fly

And they stood and watched
the big Lion come up
With a lick of his lips
he was keen as a pup

To fight the old Lion
and to take his place
He looked at Mavimba
with a grin on his face

Then he saw all the others
and he glared at each one
And not one of them moved
in that hot African sun

Not one of them moved
from their well worn seat
Not one of them moved
in the African heat

And he saw in their faces
He could not win this fight
And made off with a growl
into the coming night

With the cheers and the songs
of each bird, animal and insect
Who had come to Mavimba
to watch and protect

WHAT IS THIS STORY ABOUT?
What does it say?

Be sure always to
care for each other
our friends
our grandparents
our sister, our brother
our aunts and uncles
our father and mother

Stand together in unity
Together as one
community
No problems or worries
will ever be
too big or too small
too much, you will see

If you
stand together,
yes, stand as one
You will ALL
be winners
when the day is done

Rhino's Field

About caring and sharing

Now when young Rhinos
are just the right age
They leave their mothers
to begin a new stage

They go out to find
their very own spot
Under the African sun
so hot

So this was OUR young Rhino's mission
To find his spot – best place – best position

He jaunted along at a very good
pace
certain he would find the very
best place
He felt quite sure he would be
a Rhino with land and a GREAT
destiny

He would be Sir Rhino . . .
or Lord Rhino . . .
or
Rhino the Great . . .

President
Ruler
Head of State!

But . . .
he really
quite fancied
He quite liked
the ring
of . . .
The most splendid
most mighty . . .
'RHINO KING'!

He searched from left to right
with his horn high in the air
His head full of importance
and with individual flair

*

And so it was
that he happened to find
The most marvellous place
The very best kind

OR SO HE THOUGHT ...

It appeared before him
out of the blue
A beautiful field
all fresh, green and new

Luscious long grass, always good to eat
Leafy green bushes, good shade from the heat
And the perfect ditch
with perfect sand
To rub and to roll in
The very BEST piece of land

Said Rhino,
'This is a field
fit for one thing ...
The home of the most
splendid ... most mighty ...
RHINO KING'

And he shook himself up
with regal pride
Measured his field,
this far and so wide

This was HIS spot
this was where he would stay
He'd be its ruler
and he'd rule it HIS way!

He postured and puffed
with regal air
Flounced and bounced
with individual flair

Then something caught his eye
It bothered him
He was not sure why
But right slap-bang
in the middle of his land
Stood a curious hill
of caramel coloured sand

Cautiously he approached
the sandy mound
Something was there
a movement, a sound

And he thought as he
looked, he was
NOT AT ALL
PREPARED
To have anything to do
with anything shared

He sniffed and snorted
all around
'til he came upon
several holes in the ground

As he stared down one
he heard a sniggle
Then a funny sound
a kind of a giggle

His brow crumpled up
in a curious frown
As he lowered his eye,
tried to peer further
down

The giggle became a laugh
that shook the whole mound
Rhino stumbled back
in fright at the sound

As just at that moment
with shrieks of great mirth
A whole family of Meerkats
popped out of the earth

And to his surprise,
his horror, his shock
In fits of laughter
they began to mock

All his posturing
and flouncing
Puffing up and
regal bouncing

They marched
around
in full
Rhino parade
Oh, what a sight
in the bushveld
they made

And they laughed and
laughed and laughed all the
more
As Rhino grew mad
then madder ...
then madder
than before

Then he drew himself back
larger than large
And thundered into a full
Rhino charge

48

But before he could reach them
the Meerkats had gone
He charged around
but he couldn't find one

He could still hear their laughter
from under the mound
As the dust grew thick
from his stomping around

But when the dust
finally settled
Cleared right away
Oh what a sight! There
Rhino lay

Bottom in the air,
chin in the muck
One front
and one back leg
firmly stuck
down the Meerkat holes
he'd trampled around
With the Meerkats
still laughing
from under the ground

It was just then
that the Oxpecker bird
swooped down
from the sky
(Now Oxpecker birds are
not generally shy)
She had spotted Rhino
as he lay there stuck
Bottom in the air,
chin in the muck

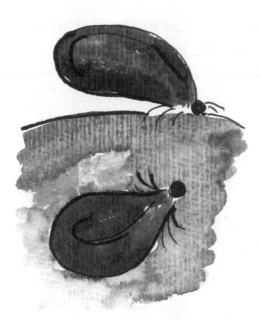

At first she had only one
thing in mind
The fat, juicy ticks she
hoped
to find
On Rhino's round, stuck
out behind

Now Oxpeckers think
ticks
are a treat
The best kind of treat
in the African heat

All chewy and gooey
and bleak inside
A delicious treat
from the Rhinoceros's hide

But, because Oxpeckers are very polite
She first had to find out
if Rhino was all right
She said, 'My dear Rhino,
things have gone a bit round the bend
You seem to be in need
of a good Rhino friend'

And with instructions like
'Move a little here, then there
Then a little towards me'
Rhino set his front leg free

The laughter from the mound suddenly stopped
And slowly but surely the Meerkats popped
out of their holes in the ground
To gather around on top of their mound

Said Oxpecker sternly
'You all had a hand in this, I have no doubt
So now you can help me to sort it all out'

'Come on then, each one of you
If we work together, it might just do
Pull from the front, and push from the rear
You push and pull, and I will steer'

'First pull!
Now push!
Now push and pull!'
And together they freed
the young Rhino bull

Rhino stood, shaken and forlorn
He couldn't even raise his great Rhino horn

Then the Oxpecker said
'Come on, you great lout
Don't you understand
what this is all about?'

'If you want this lovely field
then you're going to have to share
You have to understand
and you have to be fair'

'If you think you're more important
then you're quite wrong
We all have to learn
how to get along'

From that day on Rhino shared his land
Shared his grass and his fine patch of sand
And never again did the Meerkats tease him

In fact they went
out of their way
to please him
They found him
the best grass
– every day –
without fail
They scratched
his back
and brushed his tail

And the Oxpecker bird
got to eat all the ticks
That every Oxpecker
pecks and picks

All chewy and gooey
and black inside
A de-licious treat
from the
Rhinoceros's hide

WHAT IS THIS STORY ABOUT?
What does it say?

Share your things
your toys, your space
Let others feel
they, too, have a place

Remember ...
we all belong to
ONE
human race

Footnote:
Rhinos are very territorial in the
wild African bush.
They defend their patch of land
fiercely, and charge, with grim
determination, at
any unsuspecting trespasser.

The Pompous Elephant

About how no one person is better than another

Elephant said to the Toad
'Will you walk a while with me
There are many different things
I want you to see'

'Here in the African veld
under the hot African sun
Live many wild animals
and I'm number one'

'Mmm ...'
said the Toad

'Over there is Hippo, round
and large
Be careful, if you stop now
she might charge'

'Wallowing in waterholes
she's just so lazy
Eating those pond plants
well, that's just crazy'

'Mmm ...'
said the Toad

'Then over there
Tortoise sits
Eating teeny, tiny bits'

'He's so small
on the
bushveld ground
How can he be seen
if he
doesn't make
a sound?'

'Mmm ...' said the Toad

'And here comes Butterfly
Oh let her flutter by
She does nothing much else
you know'

'And if you ask me,
well, if you ask me'

(whisper)
'I think she's only for show!'

'Mmm ...'
said the Toad

'Oh! And then
there's Rhino'

'Ah, but what
do I know
He stamps out
fires they say'

'With those hard
heavy heels
there can't
be much
that he feels'

'And
I'm sure he doesn't
mean to
anyway!'

'Mmm ...'
said the Toad

'Over there sits Lion
Oh so snooty
Handles himself with a
great sense of duty'

'What do they say?
Ha!
He's the
King of the Jungle'

'What about me?
Someone's made
a bungle'

'Mmm ...'
said the Toad

'Me, I am as fierce,
as fierce as the best'

'In fact, quite a lot
better than the rest'

'And … OH NO!!
What's that?'

'Oh my hat!
Oh my hat!'

'Can it be?
Can it be?'

'Oh no, no … no
not
that!'

And off he rumbled
And off he stumbled
in panic …
fast!

Toad watching him disappear
said at last

'Mmm ...
You're as large as a house
and you're scared of a ...

MOUSE!'

'Mmm ...'

said the 'Toad

WHAT IS THIS STORY ABOUT?
What does it say?

Sometimes we may think
we are better than others
Let's all remember that
we are
sisters and brothers

And no one is more
and no one is less

We ALL have our faults
Me too, I confess

Footnote:
The African elephant, as large as he is,
is in fact very much afraid
of the little African field mouse.
He becomes startled and agitated
and heads off as
fast as he can.

Jackal's Nasty Words

About saying sorry and forgiving

Now Jackal was a crafty fellow
There he was, all black,
brown and yellow

He'd sneak about
and listen in on
Weasel around
and try something
to pin on
anyone he could

He'd go from one to the next
telling nasty tales
Like how Lion had such
dirty nails

And how Porcupine
had no spine

He'd say nasty things
behind their backs
Always making sure
that he
covered his tracks

And so one day ...
Jackal began talking
to Bushpig
About Tortoise's walking

'Have you seen her?' Jackal said
'Moves her feet, but not her head'

'Isn't her walk, so without style?
To get anywhere takes such a long while'

And Bushpig just nodded
but didn't feel good
And tried not to listen
as much as he could

But really he should just have said
'STOP!'

'I don't want to listen any more to your chatter
Talking about others, it really does matter'

'I WON'T talk about others
it doesn't make me feel good
I DON'T think it's kind
and I don't think that you should'

But he didn't say that
instead he just sat

Then Jackal spoke to Tortoise
about Bushpig

'With so little hair
he needs a bush wig'

Oh how Jackal would laugh
and cackle and snigger
About how Bushpig's tusks
should be a lot bigger

And Tortoise just nodded
but didn't feel good
And tried not to listen
as much as she could

But really she should just have said
'STOP!'

'I don't want to listen any more
to your chatter
Talking about others
it really does matter'

'I WON'T talk about others
it doesn't make me feel good
I DON'T think it's kind
and I don't think that you should'

But instead she just sat

Then one day
Tortoise overheard
Jackal talking to Secretary Bird

'Have you seen Tortoise?'
Jackal said
'Ha, ha, moves her feet but not her head
Ha, ha, she can't even walk in a straight line
She doesn't have fast legs like mine'

Tortoise listened to Jackal talk
All about her funny walk
Tortoise's heart began to hurt badly
She tucked herself into her shell
and cried sadly

And so Bushpig found her
A wet patch around her

'What is the matter?'
he asked in concern

And so Bushpig was to learn
All about what Jackal had said
About the walk, the small tusks
and bald head

'Oh, that nasty Jackal!' Bushpig exclaimed
'He's so nasty and rude
He should be ashamed!'

'To talk about others in such a bad way
I wish I'd not listened to what he'd to say'

'I'm sorry I did, please forgive me
Listening to nastiness is wrong
you agree?'

Said Tortoise ...
'That is very true
I'm sorry Bushpig, I listened too
Oh dear, oh dear, what shall we do?'

Said Bushpig
'My dear friend
I wish I knew'

But they didn't notice that Jackal was near
listening in with his fine tuned ear
And as he heard what they were saying
he realised the game he'd been playing

He realised that it was bad
to say the nasty things he had

He went right over
to Tortoise
and said,
'Please don't worry
I overheard you,
and I'm sorry'

'To talk about others is wrong
now I see
Please, please, please forgive me'

Tortoise waited a moment in thought
Had a lesson really been taught?
Then it came uncontrollably
'You are forgiven,'
she said nobly

Then Jackal turned to Bushpig
to ask the same
Bushpig saw clearly
Jackal's shame
'Yes, I forgive you,'
Bushpig said at last
'Now let us all forget the past'

Said Jackal,
'I would like to make amends
From now on, can we all be friends?'

WHAT IS THIS STORY ABOUT?
What does it say?

When we talk about others
behind their back
It really is good manners WE lack
Yes, it is rude and nasty and sad
And when we listen
it's just as bad
But you can say sorry, apologise
Make amends
that is wise

Forgiveness is the key they say
For you to start
a brand new day

Footnote:
In the African bush, the jackal is a notorious
thief. Cunning and clever,
he will sneak about and steal food
right from under the lion's nose
He always seems to know
exactly what is going on in the African bush.

Giraffe Who Stuck His Neck Too Far Out

About learning that rules are there to keep us safe

Now in the Bushveld
you really must know
How to quietly
go with the flow

Not to stamp and shout
and thrash about
But to glide through the bush,
as quiet as can be
Not to attract attention,
you see

There are Lions and Leopards
that can catch you
Cheetahs and Wild Dogs
that can snatch you

And in the murky waters deep
Crocodiles lie half asleep

Always watching who goes by
Quietly in wait they lie
For the unsuspecting stranger
who isn't careful
of the danger

So there are some rules
that help you melt
into the bush
of the African veld

Like keeping away from open spaces
Rather hiding in bushy places

Staying downwind
so Lion can't smell you
These are a few of the rules
I can tell you

But when you go down to drink
Be careful
and always think
of the most important rule

Do not drink too far
into the pool

Now young Giraffe
was taught the rules
Especially those about drinking
at pools

But he said . . .

'My neck is long,
I can see danger coming
My legs are strong,
I can beat them by running'

'One kick
from me
will send them
flying
One knock
from me
will send them
off crying'

'I can stamp
and shout
and
thrash about'

'No one can
catch me
No one can
scold me'

'No one can match me
No one can hold me'

But he had forgotten the crocodiles ...

Half asleep in the murky deep
Quietly waiting

Always watching

Ready to snatch

Ready to catch
anyone who had forgotten the rule

Do not drink too far
into the pool

Now Giraffe felt he needed a drink
And crashed his way
to the very brink
Of the very waterhole
where the crocodiles lay

(They had not had a meal that day)

Hungry, they waited in the cool
For someone to forget the rule

Do not drink too far
into the pool

Giraffe bent his knees
and stooped down low

Dipping his head,
he did not know
That as he slurped and burped
and squelched and belched
all the water he could drink

The crocodiles
had approached
the brink!

Giraffe was still quite
unaware
of the danger
lurking there

And ... to reach
the clear water
further from shore
He stretched
his head out
a little more ...

The water was delicious
fresh and tasty
He stretched still further
a little hasty

Because ...

Quick as a flash, the crocodiles lunged
Like bolts of lightning, the crocodiles plunged
Towards Giraffe's
outstretched head

Now did the crocodiles get fed?

Well, just at that moment
Giraffe lifted his head
Saw the crocs
and his heart stopped dead

He pulled his head away
not a second too late
Jumped to his legs
at such a great rate
Leaped back with all his might
Just about died of fright

So just, just, in the nick of time
Just before the crocs could dine
On tasty Giraffe at their table
Off made Giraffe
As fast as he was able

And he never again forgot the rule

Do not drink too far
into the pool

He avoided water
as much as he could
Just in case the crocs made good
And finally caught him
for their lunch
(They were a very persistent bunch)

They would snap their jaws
when he walked near
And as he ran off
You could hear them jeer

'There's Giraffe
who stuck his neck
too far out
And learnt a big lesson
all about
following the most important rule'

'Do not drink too far
into the pool'

WHAT IS THIS STORY ABOUT?

What does it say?

There are many important rules
Like how to behave around
swimming pools
How to cross roads
and tie our shoelaces
And how to behave
in different places

And when we act bolder
than bold
And just like Giraffe
we don't do as we're told
We stick our necks
a bit too far out
And learn what danger's
all about

So safety first
and always stay calm
Rules are there
to keep us from harm
And if there is an emergency
Call an adult
to come and see

Hyena's Laugh

About accepting differences

Hyena had a reputation
He was known
in the animal nation
As an animal
who was a bit of a clown
He was always looked at
with a bit of a frown

He played the fool
in a terrible way

And all
the animals
had a good
bit to say

He tickled
and teased them
Punched
and squeezed them

Jumped up and down and
acted quite silly
Picked on the animals
willy nilly

Generally made their heads
ache with the pain

Of his bounce
and his pounce

And his laugh
insane

Yes, Hyena's laugh
was really quite weird
His laugh was what
they really feared

He cackled
and cavorted
Smackled
and snorted
His legs all
a-quiver
he would start
to shiver

And then
out would burst
an incredible sound

Something like
the howl of a hound
And the whoop
of a monkey
mixed together

It was a laugh
you'd remember
forever

And soon it was
that the day would come
When all the animals
would be done

With Hyena's bounce
and Hyena's pounce
With his quiver
and his shiver

But most of all
with his laugh insane
They could ... no longer ... bear the pain

So it happened one day
. . .

Fox mentioned
to Hare
that he had
a plan

Hare mentioned
to Springbok
who upped
and ran

Over
to Cheetah
and mentioned
it too

And so
to everyone
the awful
plan
flew

They would stop Hyena
from playing the fool
By throwing him into
the muddy pool

But where was Hyena?
Nobody knew
It seems he had
something
else to do

Well ...
Hyena was already down at the pool
Sitting and staring into the muddy cool

And as he looked down, dropped a tear
And cried a little
Too soft to hear

Then out of his mouth
Came a really loud groan
That soon became a really loud moan

It grew ...
and grew
louder than loud

And eventually drew the
WHOLE animal crowd

Hyena sobbed and sobbed
and howled and howled

Then Lion raised his great head and spoke

'Come on, we must help this bloke
Come on we must help this fellow'
As Hyena continued to
bellow and bellow

Said Lion
'Let's change our plan
and do something
better
I think it's time
we ALL got wetter'

And with that he jumped
into the muddy pool
And started to flop about
playing the fool

He cackled and cavorted
Smackled and snorted

He started to shake
and let himself shiver
He let his legs go
and he started to quiver

Then out from Lion came a laugh so loud
That it infected the entire crowd
They all jumped into the muddy pool
And started to flop about
playing the fool

They bounced and pounced
and laughed insane

Hyena stopped
his surprise was plain

He looked at them all in the muddy pool
covered in mud and playing the fool

And ...
his legs started to shiver
then he started to quiver

And out burst his laughter into the din
And every one shouted
'JUMP IN, JUMP IN'

In he jumped
laughing with glee
And they ALL laughed together
All loud and free

From that day on
Hyena stopped bouncing

From that day on
Hyena stopped pouncing

He no longer felt lonely because
Everyone liked him
just as he was

And EVERYONE laughed
and had such fun
In the hot
beautiful
African sun

WHAT IS THIS STORY ABOUT?

What does it say?

Accept people's differences
and you may
Find you enjoy them,
when all's said and done
Laugh and play together
and you ALL will have fun

Footnote:
The hyena is the nuisance of the bush.
He steals food, pesters lions, cheetahs
and leopards for their prey.

But the sound he makes is by far the
most distinctive thing about him
He is heard, mostly at night.
A type of lunatic laugh that makes the
hair on the back of your neck stand up
as it resonates through the African night.